SNOW WHITE

A Story of Friendship

Adapted by Lynne Roberts
Illustrated by the Disney Storybook Artists

Published by Louis Weber, C.E.O., Publications International, Ltd.
7373 North Cicero Avenue, Lincolnwood, Illinois 60712

Ground Floor, 59 Gloucester Place, London W1U 8JJ

Customer Service: 1-800-595-8484 or customer_service@pilbooks.com

www.pilbooks.com

p i kids is a registered trademark of Publications International, Ltd.

Manufactured in China.

8 7 6 5 4 3 2 1

ISBN-13: 978-1-4127-6775-0

ISBN-10: 1-4127-6775-X

Once there was a sweet princess named Snow White. She sang to the wishing well to ask for her true love to find her.

That very day, a handsome prince rode onto the castle grounds. He took one look at Snow White and instantly fell in love.

But Snow White's evil stepmother, the Queen, was jealous of Snow White's beauty. Every day, the Queen asked her Magic Mirror, "Who is the fairest one of all?"

And every day, the Queen's Magic Mirror answered, "You are the fairest one, my Queen." Then one day, unexpectedly, the Magic Mirror said something else. It said that Snow White was the fairest. It said that nothing could hide Snow White's true beauty.

The Queen was angry. She ordered her Huntsman to take Snow White into the forest. He was to make sure that she never came back.

The Huntsman was sad. "Snow White," he said, "you must run far away and hide from the Queen!"

Snow White ran as fast as she could through the forest. She was scared and all alone. She didn't know where to go. Snow White began to cry.

Out of the trees came gentle woodland animals. A kind bunny family hopped toward her. *Tweet, tweet, tweet,* sang sweet bluebirds. The animals wanted to help Snow White, so they led her past a stream, down a path, and right to a little cottage.

"It's like a doll's house," Snow White said. *Knock, knock,* Snow White tapped on the door. When no one answered, she let herself in.

Inside the cottage, Snow White found seven little plates and seven little chairs. She thought that seven children lived alone in the cottage because it was such a mess.

She wanted to do something nice for the seven children, so with help from the animals, she cleaned every corner of the tiny house. She dusted, scrubbed, and swept away the mess.

It didn't take long for Snow White to tidy up the little cottage. "I'm so sleepy," she said. She climbed the steps and found seven little beds all in a row. Each bed had a name carved into it. The names were Doc, Happy, Sneezy, Dopey, Grumpy, Bashful, and Sleepy.

"I'll take a little nap," she said with a yawn.

Bashful
Sleepy

After a hard day at the diamond mine, the Seven Dwarfs came home from work. When they walked into their cottage, something seemed strange. The cottage had been cleaned! They could not believe their eyes.

"Look, the floor has been swept," Doc said.

"Our cobwebs are missing," Sneezy said.

Suddenly, they heard a very strange sound. It came from upstairs. They bravely tiptoed up the creaky steps to their bedroom.

Snow White was just waking up when she saw the Seven Dwarfs peering at her. "You're little men! How do you do? I'm Snow White."

Snow White explained why she had run away from the Queen. The Dwarfs promised to help her.

Back at the castle, the Queen went to her Magic Mirror. The mirror said that Snow White was still more beautiful than she. It told her that Snow White was living in the cottage of the Seven Dwarfs.

The Queen was furious! She disguised herself as a peddler woman and made a special apple that would make Snow White sleep forever. The only thing that would wake her was love's first kiss.

"One taste of the apple, and her eyes will close forever," the Queen cackled.

The next morning, the Seven Dwarfs left for work. Before they went, they warned Snow White to watch out for strangers.

Snow White said good-bye to her friends and promised she would not let anyone in the cottage.

Later, there was a loud knock at the door. It was an old peddler woman, and she was selling apples. Snow White did not know that the peddler was the evil Queen, so she invited the old woman into the cottage. Then the Queen tricked Snow White into biting the poisoned apple. After just one bite of the apple, Snow White fell into a deep sleep.

The animals ran to warn the Dwarfs about what was happening. The Dwarfs hurried home as fast as they could, but they were too late. They chased the wicked Queen into the woods, and she was never seen again.

The Dwarfs were sad. They loved Snow White. She was a good friend to them. They would have done anything to save her.

The Seven Dwarfs made a bed in the forest and sat by her side every day.

The Prince heard of the sleeping girl and thought she might be Snow White. He rode his horse into the woods to find his true love.

When the Prince saw Snow White, he kissed her, and she opened her eyes! The Seven Dwarfs and the animals were overjoyed. They knew their friend's wish had finally come true!

Snow White: A Story of Friendship

A friend is someone you enjoy spending time with. It's someone who makes you feel good about yourself. Friendship is the relationship between friends. Friendship is very important, especially in times of trouble.

Snow White was kind, gentle, and caring. Those are all good qualities to have in a friend. It's no wonder then that when Snow White was in trouble, her friends rushed to help her. Everyone from the Queen's servant to the woodland animals to the Seven Dwarfs — even Grumpy! — cared about Snow White and did all they could do help her be safe and happy. After all, that's exactly what friends are for!